MELTWATER

When Nina's husband, Carl, dies in a skiing accident she feels that she'll never recover. Carl's twin sister, Ingrid, persuades Nina not to sell the riding stables that she and Carl built up. But whilst the horses help her through the grief — Nina's heart is still frozen. Then along comes Oliver, a motherless child, who communicates far better with horses than people. Nina teaches Oliver to ride but can Oliver and his father, Stewart, teach Nina to live again?

DELLA GALTON

◆

MELTWATER

Complete and Unabridged

LINFORD
Leicester

First published in Great Britain in 2002

First Linford Edition
published 2012

British Library CIP Data

Galton, Della.
   Meltwater.- -(Linford romance library)
   1. Love stories.
   2. Large type books.
   I. Title II. Series
   823.9'2–dc23

   ISBN 978–1–4448–1215–2

Published by
F. A. Thorpe (Publishing)
Anstey, Leicestershire

Set by Words & Graphics Ltd.
Anstey, Leicestershire
Printed and bound in Great Britain by
T. J. International Ltd., Padstow, Cornwall

This book is printed on acid-free paper

1

'I'm leaving your father.' Mum's voice on my answerphone was as clear as the winter sky outside my bungalow window, but I still couldn't believe I'd heard her right. I pressed rewind and played the message again.

'Hi, Nina, I just thought you ought to know I'm leaving your father.'

That was it. No preamble, no explanation. She didn't even sound overly concerned about it. What kind of a message was that to leave on my answerphone at eight o'clock on a Saturday morning? Sometimes I could have happily throttled my mother.

Picking up the phone, I pressed the memory button that stored my parents' number. Let it ring ten, twelve, fourteen times. No answer. Yet she'd only left that message twenty minutes ago. I'd been out doing the horses' morning feeds, as she'd known I would be. My parents weren't early birds. They weren't even normally up at this time of day. Perhaps she'd already left Dad and he didn't know because he was still in bed asleep. My mind raced through the possibilities. I was about to try again when the phone rang. I snatched it up.

'Mum?'

'No, it's me, Ingrid,' came the clear, bright voice of my sister-in-law. 'Sorry, have I called at a bad time? I've been trying to catch you for a couple of days.'

'You're OK.' I sighed. 'Mum just left a bit of an odd message on my answerphone, that's all.'

'What sort of an odd message?'

'Well, what she actually said was that she was leaving my dad.'

'You mean getting a divorce?' I could hear the surprise in her voice. 'I didn't realise they were having problems, your parents?'

'They're not — well, at least I didn't think they were. I've probably got the wrong end of the stick.'

'Maybe they've just had a row or something?'

'Yes, that must be it,' I said, although that seemed almost as unlikely as them splitting up. As far as I knew, my parents didn't have rows. Mum told Dad what to do and he did it. It had been the same for as long as I remembered. 'I expect I'll find out soon enough,' I said thoughtfully. 'Anyway, what were you trying to get hold of me for?'

'Just about the arrangements for Tuesday.' She hesitated. 'I'm going to the remembrance garden on my way home from work and I wondered if you'd like me to pick you up on my way by.'

'Yes, please, if you don't mind.'

'Of course I don't mind. It's easier, isn't it, if we go together?'

'Yes. Yes it is. Thanks.' I swallowed. I'd been trying not to think about Tuesday. The first anniversary of Carl's death — my husband and Ingrid's twin brother. Sometimes it felt as though he'd been gone forever. I had moments of panic when I couldn't remember the details of his face. At other times, it seemed as though no time at all had passed. I still turned over in bed, reaching for him.

'Are you OK?' Ingrid asked.

'Yes. Yes, I'm fine.'

'The other thing,' she continued, 'was that I wanted to ask you if Stewart Taylor ever got hold of you about booking a riding lesson for Oliver. You remember me telling you about little Oliver in my class? The kiddie with the problems?'

'They're coming this morning,' I said, relieved at the change of subject. 'Pop in for a coffee if you're free later and I'll tell you how it went.'

'I'd like that. See you then.'

I put the telephone down and pressed redial without much hope. Still no answer from my parents. They lived two hundred miles away, which had its advantages, but it also meant I couldn't just nip round and find out what was going on. Not that I could have dropped everything anyway. Not with five horses to look after and a day of people booked in for lessons.

I hovered by the phone for a bit longer, but it stayed silent. Eventually I gave up, pulled my woollen hat back on, buttoned up my wax jacket and went outside again. It was a bright, icy morning, the sky an arc of blue over my head. My breath puffed in the air as I crossed the lane back to the stable yard, which was a five-second walk from the bungalow Carl and I had bought five years ago. I'd been tempted to sell up and move away when he'd died. Away from this Dorset village and all the memories it held, maybe somewhere a bit closer to my parents in Cornwall. I hadn't thought I'd be able to bear staying where there were so many echoes of Carl. So many ghosts.

It had been Ingrid who'd persuaded me not to. 'You can't sell the horses,' she'd said, her voice sharp with grief.

'It's not what he'd have wanted. You know it isn't.' She'd looked at me with the same blue eyes as her brother and added more softly, 'He had two great loves in his life: you and the horses. You might think it's impossible, but it is the horses that will keep you sane. Believe me.'

Ingrid had been right, I thought, as I picked my way across the frozen mud in the field and broke the ice on the water trough. The horses had kept me sane. The routines of looking after them, the sheer physical hard work of them, had kept the structure from crumbling completely from my life.

I put out some piles of hay. The grass wasn't much good at this time of year — not enough nutrition for my two thoroughbred crosses, Anton and Buska, or the two horses that belonged to a couple in the village. They hardly rode in winter, just kept their horses at full livery. That meant they paid me to do everything, including ride them, which suited me fine. Not because I needed the money — that was one problem I no longer had — but because then I didn't have to talk about trivia. I'd never been very good at small talk; Carl had been all the social life I'd needed.

Ingrid said I was in danger of turning into a recluse. 'You never go out, you never mix with anyone,' she told me often. 'You can't hide yourself away forever, you know.'

'I teach four days a week,' I'd protested. 'I see plenty of people.'

'That's not the same,' she'd said. 'You're not going to meet anyone teaching.'

'I don't want to meet anyone,' I'd said stubbornly.

'I'm not suggesting you jump head-long into another relationship,' she'd said. 'But you could do with making some friends, Nina. It's not good for you to spend so much time alone.'

It had been Ingrid who'd persuaded me to give Oliver a riding lesson. I didn't usually teach kids. She was a primary-school teacher and he was in her class. Apparently he'd become very withdrawn when his mother had walked out on his father and him six months earlier.

'He's only eight. Far too young to lose his mum.' Ingrid's voice had been indignant. 'I'm very worried about him. He used to be such a bright little thing and now he hardly speaks. I've had a word with his dad — nice man — and apparently the only thing he shows any interest in is horses.'

I'd been sceptical at first, half-suspicious that Ingrid was more interested in me meeting Oliver's father than me teaching Oliver to ride, but eventually I'd given in. Ingrid could be very persistent when she wanted something and, besides, I knew I wouldn't have coped without her this last year. It would have seemed churlish refusing to do this one small thing in return.

I went back to the stables and changed the horses' night rugs for their day ones, fumbling with buckles and clips. Everything was harder work when it was cold. Then I put them all out in the field, except Leah, the pony that Oliver would ride for his first lesson. I leaned on the gate, watching for a moment as the horses milled around the field, ears flattening, tails swishing, snorting white plumes of breath into the air as they sorted out whose pile of hay was whose.

Then I went back home to check the answerphone. There was a message from my three o'clock lady, cancelling because she had a cold, but there was nothing else from Mum and there was still no answer when I tried phoning her. I didn't even know the numbers of any of their friends, but then I suppose that wouldn't have helped much. I could hardly have just phoned up and said, 'Hey, what's this about Mum and Dad splitting up?'

I stood in the kitchen warming my hands on the Aga and thought about the last time I'd spoken to Mum. It had been two, possibly three weeks ago. She'd been moaning about Dad then, I thought, frowning. Something about him mooching around the house and never helping her with anything. Mum had always been houseproud, but according to Dad she'd got worse since he'd retired two months previously.

'I'm not even allowed in some rooms until after four o'clock,' he'd grumbled, when she'd finally handed the phone over so he could speak to me. 'She makes me wear my slippers everywhere. Can you believe that?'

I'd laughed. 'She doesn't mean it, Dad.'

'Oh yes, she does. If I've got my gardening clothes on, she puts a piece of newspaper on the kitchen chair before I'm allowed to sit on it.' He'd lowered his voice and added, 'She's obsessed, Nina. Obsessed with cleaning.'

'I expect she's just adjusting to you being around more,' I consoled, and he'd sighed and said, 'I hope you're right. I don't know if I can stand this much longer.'

Mum's message couldn't be anything to do with that, surely, I thought, glancing round my messy kitchen. I took after Dad where tidiness was concerned. There was mud on the floor by the back door, a pile of plates in the washing-up bowl from last night and you could hardly see the table for bits of paper. The stable yard was immaculate, but I didn't bother with the house much. No one except Ingrid ever came round anyway.

It was odd though that I couldn't get in touch with either of my parents. I glanced at my watch. I couldn't afford to hang around for much longer. I had five stables to muck out and I had to get Leah ready for Oliver Taylor's lesson.

As I brushed out the pony's long, grey tail, I wondered what the little boy would make of her. She was elderly, sweet and confidence inspiring. She'd belonged to Ingrid and Carl when they were kids and neither of them could bear to part with her, even though she was twenty seven and semi-retired.

Stewart and Oliver Taylor turned up early. I didn't know what I'd been expecting, but it wasn't the brand new car that drew into the yard. Stewart Taylor wasn't what I'd expected either, I thought, studying him discreetly as he slammed the car door and bent to say something to his son. Dark-haired and broad-shouldered, he was what Ingrid would have called a hunk, and again I wondered uneasily if she was trying to match-make. It wouldn't do her any good, I thought, as the two of them walked across the parking area towards the yard. I was happy as I was, with the horses, my untidy bungalow and my memories of Carl. I didn't need anything else in my life, whatever Ingrid might think.

Stewart Taylor looked like a farmer, but he wasn't dressed like one. He wore pale jeans and white trainers. He'd regret that, I thought. It wasn't as cold as it had been earlier and the mud was thawing out fast. In contrast, Oliver was dressed sensibly in what looked like brand-new riding clothes and boots that must have cost his father a fortune. I hoped he'd be as keen on horses after his first lesson.

I went to meet them. 'Mr Taylor?' I held out my hand.

'Stewart, please,' he said, taking it. His eyes, which were surrounded by laughter lines, were a warm hazel.

'You must be Oliver.'

The child nodded and stared at the ground.

'Remember what I said, Oliver?' Stewart glanced at me rather apologetically. 'Sorry. He's a bit shy.'

'Perhaps you'd like to come and meet the pony you'll be riding?' I said. 'Her name's Leah.'

Again, no response.

'Oliver.' Stewart's voice was sharp.

This, I thought, looked like it was going to be hard work. 'She's tied up in the yard over there,' I said. 'Want to come and say hello?'

The child still didn't answer, but he

did at least look at me and it might have been a trick of the light, but I thought I saw something flicker in his eyes.

'Ever been on a horse before?'

He shook his head and I smiled encouragingly.

'Is it best if I stay or go?' his father asked.

'It's up to you,' I said, keeping my voice neutral and trying to think of a tactful way of telling him it would be better if he went. The last thing I wanted was an audience, especially as I had a feeling that this lesson was not going to go as planned. If Oliver couldn't even bring himself to speak to me, how would he find the courage to get on Leah's back? Even if he did, I was going to have trouble communicating with him.

I glanced at Stewart's white trainers and inspiration struck. 'It's quite muddy out there, though. And we probably won't be doing anything too exciting. Not on his first lesson.'

'I won't stay then.' He sounded

14

relieved. 'Don't want to put the lad off. What time shall I pick him up?'

'About twelve-fifteen?' I smiled at him with a lot more confidence than I felt. 'Don't worry, we'll be fine, Oliver, won't we?'

Oliver wasn't looking at me. He was staring over the gate at Leah, who waited patiently in the stable yard. It was hard to tell from his expression whether he was excited about the impending lesson or terrified.

'See you later, then,' his father said and climbed, rather hurriedly, I thought, back into the car. I waited until he'd driven out of the gate before I turned my attention back to Oliver. He was an attractive child, with the same hazel eyes as his dad, but his hair was fair, almost blond. Perhaps he'd inherited that from his mum, I thought, and wondered fleetingly what could have happened to have made her want to abandon her husband and child. Stewart Taylor didn't look like a wife-beater. But then I supposed you couldn't judge by appearances. Ingrid

15

had told me it was often the nicest parents who turned out to be child abusers or serial bigamists.

'Oliver was fine before she went, but he's just gone in and in since then,' she'd explained. 'It would be great if learning to ride got him interested again.'

I glanced at him now and felt a little rush of compassion. It must be hellish having your mother walk out on you when you were only eight. Mum's message on my answerphone had been enough of a shock, and I was thirty-four and knew she probably didn't mean it. I held out my hand to Oliver. 'So, shall we go and meet Leah, then?'

After a moment's hesitation, he took it and I felt a surge of relief.

'Rule number one,' I said, as we went into the yard. 'Always approach horses from the front. That way they can see you and you won't startle them. OK?'

He stared at me.

'Want to stroke her?'

He shook his head, but I led him up

16

to Leah's head anyway. As we got closer, I could feel his hand tensing in mine. Ingrid might be a brilliant, intuitive teacher, I thought, but she'd got this one wrong. There was no way this child wanted to go on a horse. He was too scared even to touch her.

'She won't hurt you, love,' I murmured. 'She's a sweet old thing.'

He pulled his hand out of mine and for a second I thought he was going to flee — run back across the yard and out of the gate and down the lane towards the village, which was more of a town these days, with its two pubs and its busy main road. This was crazy, I thought. He was obviously terrified. I bent down a bit so that our faces were on the same level.

'Look, no one's going to make you ride her, Oliver. Not if you really don't want to.'

He gazed back at me with his huge, solemn eyes, not seeming to hear me and for a moment I wanted to hug him and tell him it would be OK, that the world wouldn't always be as scary as it seemed now. It was an odd feeling. I'd never had a maternal bone in my body, yet something about this little boy's utter vulnerability was getting to me.

Before I could say anything else, he stretched out his fingers towards Leah's nose. She blew on his fingers and he smiled and then, to my complete amazement, he bent down and blew gently back. Leah flicked her grey ears and got into the swing of things and for a few seconds the two of them blew at each other gently.

'Where did you learn to do that?' I asked, when he finally stopped. He glanced at me, but for a long while he didn't answer. He was running his fingers through Leah's thick grey mane, lifting out each strand as if it were something precious. Then he said, in little more than a whisper, 'Telly.'

I realised I'd been holding my breath while I waited for his answer. 'So do you want to get on now, then? Would you like to have a ride on her back?'

He gave the slightest incline of his head in reply.

'Are you sure, Oliver? You don't have to get on her at all. Not today. Not ever if you don't want to.'

A slightly firmer nod. It was the closest I was going to get, I thought, wondering how on earth Ingrid managed with teaching him. How did you communicate with someone who didn't speak? He didn't say a word as I showed him how to get on Leah, via the mounting block in one corner of the yard. She stood patiently as he climbed up, with a little help from me. Once on top, he wound his fingers back in her mane again.

'You're going to need to hold the reins,' I told him, gently unravelling his fingers. 'Like this. Look.'

He watched and listened and did as I said. And hence the pattern was established. For the next few minutes, I gave him instructions about how to sit and where to put his legs, which he seemed to understand. Then I clipped a lead rein onto Leah's bridle and led her out of the yard and through the gate into the outdoor school.

It was fenced off from the rest of the fields and there were chippings on the ground, so it never got too hard to ride on, even on the bleakest winter's day. White painted letters marked out the perimeter. We walked round in silence except for the creak of the saddle and the soft thud of Leah's hooves. To my surprise Oliver stayed more or less in the position I'd told him, his back like a ramrod, as he looked straight ahead of him. There was nothing on his face to indicate whether he was enjoying himself or not, but he moved naturally with the pony's rhythms. It was one of the strangest lessons I'd ever given. Not to mention the quietest.

I was half-afraid that he wouldn't want to get off but, when it was time, he took his feet out of the stirrups and slid willingly into my arms. He felt thin beneath his new riding clothes, almost fragile, and again I felt that strange tug of emotion inside me. It was odd. When we'd first got married, Carl and I had talked about maybe having children one day. But it hadn't been a burning issue for either of us, so we hadn't got round to it. Back then, of course, we'd thought we had all the time in the world. Since he'd died, I'd often wondered if we'd have done things any differently if we'd known that we hadn't.

'Did you enjoy that?' I said to Oliver, as we walked back through to the yard and I tied Leah up outside her stable in the lunch-time sunlight. 'Like to help me take her saddle and bridle off?'

I wasn't expecting an answer but, as I started to undo the girth, Oliver stepped forward, his face intent. I helped him with the heavy buckles and lifted off the saddle. Oliver pressed his face against the warm damp patch where Leah had sweated under her saddle and breathed in ecstatically.

'I used to do that when I was your age,' I told him. 'I used to think that the smell of horses was the most wonderful smell in the world.'

He didn't say anything, but he smiled at me. Only the tiniest, most fleeting of smiles, but it felt like a major breakthrough and suddenly I hoped with all my heart that he would find the words to tell his father he wanted to come again. I had a feeling that Ingrid had been right after all. Horses were Oliver's passport back to life.

★ ★ ★

'It sounds like it went well,' Ingrid said, as we sat in my kitchen later on that afternoon and sipped coffee. She tucked a strand of white-blonde hair behind her ear and grinned at me over her cup. 'When's he coming again?'

'Next Saturday, I think. His dad seemed quite keen.'

'His dad would be keen on anything to get him talking again.'

'I'm not surprised. It can't be easy. Did he just stop talking completely after his mum left them? Why did she leave anyway?'

'I don't know. I mean, it's not the sort of thing you can really ask, is it? I doubt I'd get the truth anyway. And no, Oliver didn't stop talking straight away, it happened over a few weeks. He just seemed to get quieter and quieter. He does still talk a bit, you know, just not much.' She looked at me thoughtfully. 'What did you make of Stewart Taylor?'

'I didn't see him for long. He seems all right.'

Ingrid nodded. 'I guess people do split up, don't they? So what's the news on your parents, then? Heard any more?'

'No, I haven't. To be honest, I'm quite worried, Ingrid. I still haven't managed to get hold of either of them. It's odd.'

'What will you do then?'

'Keep trying, I guess. What else can I do? I can't just leave this lot and dash off up there, can I?'

'No, I suppose you can't.'

She finished her coffee and stood up. 'Better let you get on, then.'

I stood up too and went with her to the door. We hugged briefly. 'See you on Tuesday,' she said, as we drew apart. 'Maybe after we've taken Carl some flowers we could go and have a drink or something?'

'Maybe.'

'You know he wouldn't want you to be unhappy, don't you?'

'I'm not,' I said. 'Honestly.'

She lowered her eyes. 'All right. I'm sorry, I don't mean to nag. Let me know if you hear anything from your parents.'

'I will.'

I closed the door behind her, relief surging in with the silence that filled my kitchen once more. There was a photograph of Carl on the Welsh dresser. I picked it up and looked at it for a moment. Tall and athletic, with the white-blond hair of his sister and the same clear blue eyes. They'd got their looks from their Swedish father. I was in the picture, too, standing beside him, my face tilted up to his, my long, dark hair falling down my back. Carl had one arm draped around my shoulders and he was smiling into the camera, his eyes so alive that it was impossible to believe that he no longer was.

I wished I could get Ingrid to understand that I was fine. Well, as fine as it was possible to be after losing the love of my life. I'd accepted that he'd gone, that I'd never feel completely alive again without him. What else was there to do? I blinked a couple of times and put the photograph back where it belonged.

About half an hour after Ingrid had gone, the doorbell rang. I was tempted not to answer it. I wasn't expecting anyone. But the caller was persistent and eventually I went and peered through the side window to see if I could see who it was. It looked like Mum, I saw with a little rush of shock. I opened the door and saw that it was indeed Mum, clutching a box and standing next to a vacuum cleaner.

'What on earth are you doing here?' I said. 'And what's that?'

'Didn't you get my message?'

'What message?'

'The one I left on your answer-machine telling you I was leaving your father.' The box was full of cleaning things, I saw with amazement, and, as I hesitated, she leaned round me and peered into the kitchen. 'Well, aren't you going to let me in? I can see we've got lots to do.'

I stood to one side and she brushed past me, pulling out a yellow duster and flapping it in the air like a flag. 'Bring that.' She indicated the cleaner. 'I can't carry it any further.'

Dumbstruck, I did as she said. By the time I'd put it down in the corner and closed the back door, Mum was gathering armfuls of paper off the table and polishing the area of wood she'd uncovered.

'Mum.' I went across and tried to

take the duster out of her hands, but she wouldn't let it go, just clutched it to her chest and glared at me with her strange, glittery eyes.

'I knew you'd do this. I knew you wouldn't appreciate me. You're just like your father.'

I shook my head. This was beginning to feel like some sort of dream. This woman had my mother's face, but she had someone else's eyes. My mother would never have acted like this. Something was badly wrong. Then I remembered what Dad had said about her recent cleaning obsession. Surely he hadn't meant this, had he? Had he been trying to tell me she'd gone off her rocker and I just hadn't taken it in?

'Mum,' I tried again, 'can you please sit down a minute and tell me what's going on.' I pulled out a chair at the kitchen table and eventually I persuaded her to sit in it, but she still wouldn't let go of the duster. She sat twining it round her fingers and not looking at me.

27

'Does Dad know you're here?' I said gently. 'Did he bring you?'

'Of course he didn't,' she snapped. 'I've left him, I told you.'

'But why? Why have you left him?'

'Because he's seeing someone.'

'What do you mean he's seeing someone? You've been married for forty years. Why on earth would he want to do that?'

'You tell me,' she said, 'but he is. He says he's helping her with her garden, but I know your father, Nina. I know when he's lying.'

To my distress, she started to cry. Great tears rolled down her face and she patted at them with one corner of the duster. I'd never seen my mother cry, I realised. She might be bossy and manipulative but, like Dad, she was of the stiff-upper-lip brigade.

I got up and fetched some kitchen roll. 'Here, use this.'

She looked at it disdainfully, but was eventually persuaded to relinquish the duster.

Could it be possible, I thought, with a tug of guilt, that I'd been so wrapped up in my own problems for the past year that I hadn't noticed my own parents' marriage was falling apart? I decided to try a different tack. 'So who is this woman he's been seeing them? What's her name?'

'Margaret Jameson-Smythe,' she said, without a flicker of hesitation. 'She moved in next door three months ago.'

'So he can't have been seeing her for long?' I said, trying to picture my quietly spoken father as a womaniser. 'Maybe he really is helping her with her garden?'

'Nina, I am not imagining things,' she said sharply. 'Have you ever known me to imagine things?'

'No, no of course not.' I glanced doubtfully at the cleaner in the corner of the kitchen and the box of cleaning stuff on the floor beside it. I'd never seen her like this either.

She sniffed. 'I know what you're thinking. You think I'm losing my marbles, don't you? Well, I can assure you I'm not. Your father is carrying on with that hussy from next door and so I've left him. It's as simple as that, Nina. Until I've sorted out somewhere else to live, I'm going to have to stay here with you.'

She glared at me, as if daring me to argue. I didn't. I glanced down at the duster in my hands and then back at her tear-stained face. There was absolutely nothing I could think of to say.

2

'So what are you going to do about your mum, Nina?' I could hear the concern in my sister-in-law's voice and I clenched my hands in my lap. It was just before five on Tuesday evening and we were on our way to the remembrance garden. I knew she was trying to take my mind off it.

'To be honest, I don't know,' I said at last. 'She's driving me mad. That sounds terrible, doesn't it? But the truth is we were never very good at living together at the best of times. And now she's like this.'

'You mean with her cleaning?'

I nodded and Ingrid gave me a swift, sympathetic glance, as she indicated to turn into the cemetery car park.

'Yesterday, when I came back from doing the horses, she was on her hands and knees scrubbing the kitchen floor. I nearly fell over her.'

'Sounds all right to me!'

'Yes, but I don't want my kitchen floor scrubbed. And she's moved all my papers around so I can't find anything.'

'It can't be easy.' She parked the car and turned off the ignition. 'I couldn't live with my mother, that's for sure.' She undid her seat-belt and leaned across to the back seat for the flowers. We always brought the same kind: Ingrid carnations, and me white roses. We'd stopped on the way here to get them. I held the Cellophane-wrapped bunch and bent my head to sniff them. No scent. Perfectly formed white velvet petals that smelt of nothing. It seemed wrong somehow and, fleetingly, I thought of Carl lying in the chapel of rest, his white-blond hair falling back from his handsome, chiselled face. He'd still looked tanned. Still looked as if he might open his eyes, sit up and swing his legs on to the floor. He'd looked too strong, too perfect to be dead.

'You all right?' Ingrid asked softly.

'I'm fine.' I blinked as the roses blurred in front of me. 'You?'

'Yes.' She was blinking, too, I saw. We got out of the car and stood in the early evening sunlight. It was hard to believe that a year had passed since we'd lost him. My husband and Ingrid's twin brother. A year ago today.

We went through the cemetery gates and walked up towards the remembrance garden, both of us quiet with our own thoughts. There weren't many people about. The setting sun dappled the mossy pathway and cast its clear, golden light across old stone and white marble.

The gate of the remembrance garden squeaked as Ingrid pushed it open and we walked up to the memorial stone. *Carl Andersson, beloved husband of Nina. Son of Johan and Sarah, brother of Ingrid. May 1966–November 2001.* I swallowed and looked away from the familiar words. Ingrid knelt on the grass and removed the old flowers from the plant holder within the stone. Then she dropped a small kiss on the carnations she carried before putting them in place.

'Hello, my darling,' she murmured.

I watched wordlessly. I'd never been able to speak to Carl as she did. Not here, anyway. Perhaps because there was a part of me that didn't believe he was really here. This might be where his ashes lay, what was left of his physical self, but his soul had soared from his body far from here. On a snowy mountainside in the Swedish Lapland. He'd been skiing with his Uncle Gustaf, the only relative who still lived there. Carl had died within a few miles of the place where he and Ingrid had been born.

Ingrid got up slowly, her head bowed, and I realised that I was still clutching my roses. I bent to put them beside the carnations. I would go to that mountainside one day. Maybe I'd be able to speak to Carl there, in that stark black and white landscape, so different from this peaceful garden of flowers. Maybe

I'd be able to say my goodbyes there.

As I stood up again, Ingrid held out her arms and for a moment we hugged. 'Thanks for coming with me,' I murmured.

'Don't be silly.' We drew apart and she looked at me. 'We'll never really get over him, but he wouldn't want us to be unhappy. Especially you.' Her eyes were just like Carls. The same shade of blue, the same shape. Sometimes, just for a moment, I could imagine he was looking back at me. Watching me from behind his sister's eyes. 'No more crying, then.'

'I'm not crying,' I said, wiping my face and surprised to find it wet.

She crinkled up her mouth, half grimace, half smile. 'All right. Have you time for a drink? Or do you have to get back for your mother?'

'No, I don't have to get back for a while.' I was beginning to dread going back to my bungalow, which was no longer peaceful since Mum had moved in. It would be a relief to put it off for a while longer.

'Good,' Ingrid said. 'You can tell me what's been going on over a glass of Chardonnay.'

Fifteen minutes later, we sat at a corner table in The Bat and Bottle, one of the two pubs in our village. I glanced round idly. I hadn't been in here for ages. I remembered it being a rather dingy, smoky place with nicotine-coloured walls, but it had been refurbished and updated. A large section was now a restaurant and the part we sat in was non-smoking, the walls hung with watercolours of local landscapes.

'Do you fancy anything to eat?' Ingrid asked, picking up a bar menu. 'Jacket potato? Baguette?'

'No, I'm not hungry. Anyway, I'll probably have to make Mum something when I get back.'

'How long is she staying?'

'I don't know. I've got to get her talking to Dad again, but at the moment she won't even speak to him.'

'Why not?'

'She thinks he's having an affair with the woman next door.'

'And is he?'

'I shouldn't think so. He's idolised Mum for as long as I can remember; it's bizarre.'

Ingrid rested her chin in her hands and looked at me. 'So, what does he say about it all?'

I sipped my wine and frowned. 'Actually, that's the most worrying bit. He seems quite relieved. He says it's been going on for a while, this cleaning obsession, and he can't cope with it any more.'

'So you're piggy in the middle. Oh dear.' She looked sympathetic 'What are you going to do?'

'I thought I'd wait until the weekend and see if we'd managed to sort anything out, although I don't know what. We stayed up really late last night talking, but we didn't get very far.' I took another sip of my wine. 'I wanted to get today over with.'

'Of course.'

For a few moments neither of us spoke. Then the door opened and a man came into the pub.

'That looks like Stewart Taylor,' I murmured.

Ingrid turned to look, at the same moment as a fair-haired boy came in behind him. 'Yes, it is. There's Oliver.' She smiled across at them and said to me, 'I expect they've come in for their evening meal to save cooking. He doesn't look like the cooking type, does he?'

'No,' I said, thinking again that he looked more like an outside worker than the editor of the local paper that Ingrid had told me he was. Big, but not overweight, he'd had to bend his head to avoid hitting it as he came in the door. I hoped they wouldn't come over. I didn't feel like talking to anyone except Ingrid. But they did, of course, Stewart smiling as he crossed the carpet and Oliver following, obviously reluctant.

'Hello, ladies,' Stewart said. 'Don't worry, I'm not gatecrashing. I just wanted to say thank you.' He glanced at Ingrid. 'To you for introducing me to Nina and . . . ' He turned towards me, warmth in his hazel eyes. 'To you for Saturday. He can't wait for his next riding lesson, can you, Oliver?'

Oliver chewed his lip and didn't say anything, but his father seemed unperturbed. 'They do nice food here.'

'We're not eating,' I said hastily.

'No.' A shadow crossed his face and he said, 'We'll leave you to it then. See you Saturday, Nina.'

'Nice, isn't he?' Ingrid said, as they went towards the restaurant. Then, seeing my expression, 'Look, I'm not trying to matchmake, Nina, if that's what you think. I just thought learning to ride might help Oliver.'

'I know. I'm sorry,' I said, feeling guilty. 'You were right. I think he's going to be good. And yes, his father is nice. I'm just not feeling sociable.'

She stared at me for a moment. 'I might come over for a ride myself at the weekend, if that's all right with you? We could discuss tactics for getting your mum and dad back together. Or at least a way of slowing her down on the cleaning front.'

'Yes, that would be good.'

We talked for a while longer about mothers and our ambiguous relationships with them and then Ingrid said, 'Well, I suppose I'd better drop you back, then.'

'I won't stop,' she said as she pulled up outside the bungalow. 'I'll see you at the weekend. Don't be sad, Nina.'

'I'm not.'

She touched my arm. 'Good luck with your mum.'

I'd need it, I thought as I walked up to the front door. The sound of vacuuming was coming out of the lounge window and I could feel myself tensing as I went in. The cleaner was plugged into a socket by the kitchen door, the lead stretching through to the lounge. I switched it off as I passed, then paused in the doorway and waited for my mother's reaction.

'What did you do that for?'

'You went through the whole place this morning. Why are you doing it again?'

'Because it needs it. This carpet's filthy. I don't know what you've been doing in here.' Her lips went into a thin, red line, as she dared me to argue.

'Living in it, Mum. That's what I've been doing. It's not a show house. It's my home. That's what you do in a home. Live in it.'

'There's no need to shout at me, Nina. I'm only trying to help.'

I took a deep breath. Why did she always make me feel so guilty — as if I was a naughty little girl, instead of a grown woman?

'I'm not shouting at you,' I said, knowing my voice was rising even as I spoke. 'I just don't want you cleaning up all the time. It's not necessary and it's ridiculous.'

'Oh, so I'm ridiculous now, am I? Well, that's charming.' She was wearing rubber gloves, I noticed. Pink ones that she must have brought with her. I didn't think she could have found them in my kitchen. She clutched the handle of the cleaner and glared at me. 'You've got exactly the same attitude as your father. He'd rather be slopping about outside than doing anything round the house.'

I bit back the urge to say I couldn't blame him and took a deep breath. This was getting us nowhere. 'Look, why don't you sit down and I'll make us a nice cup of tea.'

She pouted, looking more like a spoilt child than a woman in her sixties. I took this as a yes and went into the kitchen.

When I came back, she was sitting on the settee, although not directly on it. The corners of a tea-towel poked out from beneath her plaid skirt. Presumably she thought that my settee was as dirty as my carpet. I put our cups on the glass coffee table and didn't comment. Then I sat opposite her in the armchair.

'You didn't say you were going out.'

'No.' I pushed the sugar bowl towards her. I knew she hadn't remembered what day it was. For someone so organised, she was hopeless with dates, so when Ingrid had come round to pick me up, I'd just called from the back door that I wouldn't be long.

'So how's Ingrid these days? Still not married?' She was watching me over her tea-cup.

'No. She's a primary schoolteacher. She's too busy with her career.'

'Ah, well, I can't blame her for that. Marriage isn't all it's cracked up to be, you know.'

'I wish we'd had long enough to find out.' The words were out of my mouth before I could stop them. Hard and bitter. Then I was standing up and the tea was spilling everywhere, but I didn't care. I had to get out of the room. Away from the shocked look on my mother's face. Away from the sudden, wrenching pain inside me that had nothing to do with the hot tea that was seeping through my trousers.

I stumbled into my bedroom, where I ripped off my trousers and found a flannel from the bathroom to put across the red marks on my leg. Nothing serious. Nothing at all compared to the pain my mother's words had stirred within me. My heart pounded and my head was spinning from the wine and from shouting at my mother. Maybe Ingrid was right, I thought, as I sat on the bed and shivered. I pulled the duvet up round me. Maybe I hadn't got over losing Carl. Maybe I wasn't as fine as I thought.

About ten minutes later, there was a knock on the bedroom door. I didn't answer, but I knew she wouldn't go away. I was right — the door opened a crack and she poked her head around it.

'Are you all right? Did you burn yourself? I've brought you another cup of tea.'

When I still didn't answer, she came

right into the room.

'I'm sorry, Nina. I didn't realise what day it is. It is today, isn't it?' She sounded unusually hesitant, the hard lines of her face softened by the shadows of the room. 'Have you been there to see him? Is that where you and Ingrid were going?'

'Yes.'

She put the tea on the bedside table and perched on the edge of the bed. Again, I felt as though I were a child. As though she'd come to read me a bedtime story. She'd done that a lot when I was little. The memory brought a bitter-sweet mixture of emotions with it. She'd been all of my world then. How did a mother and daughter grow so far apart that they became strangers?

'Shall I leave you to it, then?'

'No, stay. Tell me about you and Dad.' I could hear my voice cracking a little.

She sighed, but made no move to go. 'You've always been happy, haven't you?'

45

'Yes and no.'

Ignoring the no, I said, 'Then you could be happy again.' Because suddenly it was terribly important that they were. So much in my life had changed during this past year, but they'd always been sound. A little oasis of stability. I had a picture of them growing old together in their nice house, with its neat kitchen, sunny patio and geraniums in window-boxes. I didn't think I could bear it to be changed.

'You bottle things up too much,' she said unexpectedly. 'You get that from me.'

I looked at her. 'Is that what you're doing with Dad?'

She shook her head and refused to say anything else, despite my protestations that everything could be sorted out if you wanted it badly enough.

* * *

Although we'd resolved nothing and I still didn't know how long she was going to stay, I felt easier with Mum after Tuesday. For the rest of the week, neither of us mentioned Dad or Carl, yet the atmosphere was lighter. It was as if something had been cleared up between us, although I couldn't put my finger on quite what.

'She's even slowed down on the cleaning front,' I told Ingrid when I rode out with her on Saturday morning. We'd gone early, because I had to be back for Oliver's lesson. There was a nip of frost in the air. Spiderwebs shone silver in the hedgerows and the sky was a great bowl of blue above our heads.

'She's probably slowed down because your bungalow's immaculate now,' Ingrid said, as she rode beside me on the bridle path. 'The kitchen floor's so shiny I nearly slipped over on it this morning.'

'That won't last long. I'll be tramping mud over it again later.'

She laughed. 'It feels good being on a horse again, you know. Although I think my legs will ache a bit tomorrow.'

'Come and do it again. That's the best cure for aching legs.'

'Pity it's not the best cure for aching hearts,' she said cryptically. We'd reached the beginning of a sloping uphill track where the horses were used to cantering and they were both dancing on the spot.

'I think they're ready for a stretch out,' I said. 'Fancy it?'

She nodded, her eyes sparkling.

Buska didn't need telling twice. As I shortened the reins, I felt him bunching up beneath me. Sheer power, just waiting for my signal. I could see that Anton, the horse Ingrid was riding, was just as keen. We charged up the hill, side by side, only stopping at the top because of an early-morning dog walker out with his three pointers.

'Wow. I enjoyed that,' Ingrid said, when she'd got her breath back. 'Blows away the cobwebs, doesn't it?'

And with the mention of cobwebs, we were back to talking about my mother once again.

'I'll speak to Dad again,' I said. 'Tonight. We'll sort something out then.'

★ ★ ★

'I think you're ready for a little trot,' I said to Oliver later that morning, as we walked around the track of the outdoor school. 'Do you fancy it?' In normal circumstances, I wouldn't have suggested it so soon, but Oliver was such a natural. He'd remembered everything from his first lesson and was moving easily with the rhythm of the pony.

Now he nodded silently, his big hazel eyes on mine.

'Rising to the trot is the hardest bit to learn,' I continued, 'but once you've mastered that, you're halfway there. I'll hold the lead rein until you get the hang of it.'

Another silent nod.

I showed him what to do and he was obviously taking it all in because he gave her the signal to trot as soon as I'd finished explaining. Leah pricked her ears and trotted beside me and Oliver bounced around on her back. His face was a study in concentration. To my amazement, after two circuits he was rising to the trot — slightly erratically as he adjusted to the rhythm, but definitely there. I asked him to stop and start a couple of times, to convince myself it wasn't just a fluke. It wasn't. I glanced at my watch. Three quarters of an hour into his second lesson. I'd never known anyone learn so fast.

'That was brilliant.' I was as breath-less as he was. 'Now let me see you go into a nice straight halt.'

He did as I said, his little face flushed with effort. I smiled at him and reflected that if we could get half as far with our talking skills as his riding ones, his father would think it was money well spent.

'You're doing really well,' I told him.

For a moment, he looked as if he was going to say something, then, to my distress, his face crumpled and he started to cry.

'Oliver. What is it? What's the matter?' Instinctively I held out my arms and he half climbed, half fell off Leah's back into them. I let go of her lead rope and cuddled him and he wrapped his skinny arms around my neck and sobbed. His whole body was shuddering, I realised. Poor little mite.

'It's OK,' I said, over and over. 'It's OK, I've got you.'

I don't know how long we stood there in the middle of the school, but when he finally stopped crying, my arms ached from holding him and Leah had wandered over to the gate and was trying to get her head under it to reach the long grass the other side.

'You sit down here a minute,' I told Oliver. 'I'd better catch that naughty pony before she runs off.'

He sat where I told him, but before I could move towards Leah, he said, in a voice little more than a whisper. 'My mum ran off. Because I was naughty.'

'Oh no, darling. That's not true. She'd never do that.' I felt the words tumbling out as I looked into his sad little face. 'Mums don't do that.'

'She did.' He picked at a loose thread on his jodhpurs. 'She told me to tidy my room and I didn't do it. And I heard her shouting at Dad and when I woke up she was gone.'

I knelt beside him. 'Listen, Oliver. It's not your fault. I promise you. Sometimes mums and dads argue, but it's because they're cross with each other, not with you.' I put my arm around him and his eyes filled with tears again.

'Naughty people get locked up. I don't want to be locked up for a long time.'

'No one's going to lock you up.'

'They will, and they'll throw away the key. I heard Dad saying it.' He buried his head in my jumper. Before I could respond, there was a shout from behind us.

'Hey — what's happened?' Stewart Taylor was over the gate and running towards us. 'He hasn't fallen off, has he?' The question was aimed at me, but he was looking at Oliver, his face anxious.

'No, nothing like that.' I scrambled to my feet, brushing chippings off my jodhpurs, suddenly embarrassed to be found in such an intimate position with his son. 'He's not hurt,' I said. 'He's fine. Well, I mean he's not fine, but . . . '

I'd barely exchanged two sentences with Stewart Taylor. How did I begin to tell him about the conversation we'd just been having?

Oliver had got to his feet, too, and was staring at the ground.

'If you don't mind holding on a minute,' I said to Stewart, 'I'll just put the pony away and I'll explain.'

He nodded, his face serious.

I caught Leah and led her back to her stable. As I took off her saddle, I heard Stewart tell Oliver to go and get in the car. Then he strode back across the yard. He didn't look very happy, I saw, with a sinking feeling in my stomach.

He leaned on the stable door and I

decided it would be best to plunge straight in and tell him the truth.

'Oliver thinks his mum left because he was naughty.' I concentrated on undoing the buckles on Leah's bridle so I didn't have to look at him. 'He's been crying his heart out and I know it's none of my business, but — well, can't you talk to him and explain it's not his fault?' I risked a glance at him, but it was as though he hadn't heard me.

An image of Oliver's tear stained face swam before me and I thought of my own mother and the distance that had sprung up between us. Somehow I had to make his father understand. I took a deep breath. 'He's obviously got the wrong end of the stick. He told me that he's scared you'll lock him up. His exact words were lock him up and throw away the key.'

This got a reaction. Stewart went white. Then he buried his head in his hands. 'My God,' he said, his voice muffled. 'So that's what this is all about.' He lifted his head and looked at me. 'There's something you ought to know, but I'd appreciate it if you kept it to yourself. I haven't even told the school. But it's for Oliver's sake. You understand?'

I nodded. I wanted to tell him that he didn't need to say anything, that his domestic affairs were nothing to do with me, but something in his eyes stopped me.

'You're right,' he murmured. 'Oliver's got completely the wrong end of the stick. He must have heard us talking. The truth is Angie — my wife — she hasn't left us. Not voluntarily.' He looked at me, his eyes bleak. 'She's in prison.'

I was so taken aback that, for a moment, I couldn't think quite what to say. But it didn't look as if Stewart wanted me to say anything. It was as if, now that he'd actually told someone, he couldn't stop the details pouring out.

'Angie was involved in embezzling some funds from the company that she used to work for.' He screwed up his face as if he still couldn't bring himself to say the words out loud. And when he spoke again, I realised why.

'She worked for a charity,' he said, 'which didn't exactly endear her to the courts, so they were harder on her than they might have been if she'd been working for an ordinary business. The only good thing that ever came out of our marriage was Oliver.' He turned towards me and there was such pain in his face that it shocked me. 'That's what Oliver overheard,' he said quietly. 'It was me who said they should lock *her* up and throw away the key.'

3

Stewart looked at me, his eyes clouded with pain, but I still couldn't think of a single thing to say that would make him feel better, although I felt an over-whelming sense of compassion for him. How hard it must have been to live with something like this, yet keep it a secret not just from the world but from his son too.

I came out of Leah's stable. It didn't seem right to still be in there with the stable door between us now that this stranger had dropped his guard so utterly to me. I picked up Leah's saddle and bridle. 'So, will your wife . . . will she be in prison for a long time?'

He nodded. 'We're paying back the money, which made it a bit better, but yes. She'll be there for some time. It wasn't her first offence, you see.'

I walked across the yard and put

Leah's saddle on the fence.

He walked beside me. 'Perhaps I should have been honest with Oliver from the start. But how do you tell a child something like this?' His face still looked grey. 'I thought it best that he didn't know. It seemed easier just to tell everyone she'd left.'

'Yes,' I murmured, wondering what I would have done in his shoes.

'The hardest part was keeping it out of the papers.'

In the car park I could see Oliver sitting in the car, his blond head bowed as he thought goodness knows what.

'That's a hire car,' Stewart said, following my gaze.

'I wasn't thinking . . . ' I broke off.

'We owned our house before all this happened,' he went on. 'We don't own very much any more. Luckily Angie's parents are very well off. Well, they were.' His mouth twisted. 'Sorry, I don't know why I'm dumping all this on you.'

'It's all right,' I told him. 'Really it is.

I mean, it must be a relief to talk about it.'

'It can't go any further.' He looked at me as if something had suddenly struck him. 'I can't risk the school finding out. Nothing like this ever stays confidential. Oliver couldn't take it.'

'It's all right,' I said again. 'I won't tell Ingrid. I won't tell a soul. Don't worry.'

He took his wallet out of his pocket and handed me two folded notes. 'Oliver's lesson?'

'He's doing really well,' I said, wondering fleetingly whether I should take his money.

'He's loves it,' Stewart said, pushing the notes into my hand. 'It's going to bring him back to me. All the money in the world couldn't make up for that.'

'But you will talk to him, won't you? Make him understand that his mum hasn't left because of him? It's talking to him that will really bring him back to you. He must have been bottling it up all this time.'

'Of course, now I know how he feels. I'll talk to him when we get home.' Stewart reached out a hand, but let it drop away before he made contact. 'Thanks, Nina. Thanks for being honest with me about that.'

My comments about his son's conversation were a drop in the ocean compared to what he'd just told me, I thought, but I just nodded.

He straightened, as if by the physical movement he was making an effort to pull himself together, to get our relationship back on a professional footing once more. 'We'll see you next week, then?' he said, and gave me a quick nod before striding towards his car.

As I walked back across the road to the bungalow, it struck me that Mum had used those words — 'bottling up' — earlier in the week. She'd said I hadn't let myself grieve for Carl. I wasn't altogether sure what she'd been getting at. I wasn't the kind of person who went to pieces in public, if that was what she meant. But then, neither was she.

I supposed we all dealt with stress in different ways. Little Oliver had gone inside himself. Mum seemed to think she could deal with her problems by cleaning everything in sight, while Dad was burying his head in the sand and trying to pretend his didn't exist. My problems seemed very small compared with Stewart Taylor's though.

I let myself into the bungalow and plonked Leah's saddle on the rack in the utility room. Then I stood by the back door, my head still reeling from all that Stewart had said. I was so wrapped up in my thoughts that for a few moments I didn't notice anything different about the bungalow. Then awareness gradually dawned. It was too silent. Too still.

'Mum?' I called, as I walked through to the lounge. Perhaps she was having a nap or something. She'd said last night that she was tired.

The lounge smelt of lavender polish,

but it was empty. The only sign of my mother was a yellow duster on the coffee table. With a growing sense of unease, I went into her bedroom. Empty too. The bed had been stripped and the sheets were neatly folded. I knew even before I went into my own room that she wouldn't be there. There was nowhere else to check. My heart began to pound as I realised that the vacuum cleaner was gone too. For whatever reason, Mum had decided to do another disappearing act, and she hadn't even left me a note.

★ ★ ★

'You look awful,' Ingrid said. 'I'll put the kettle on. Or would you like something stronger?'

'Tea will do fine.' I forced a smile. It was Saturday evening and I'd just settled the horses for the night. I hadn't even had time to get changed yet, but Ingrid had come round as soon as I'd phoned and told her that Mum had gone AWOL. I hadn't been planning to tell her, but I was now seriously worried. I'd been trying Dad all day and he was either out or not answering his phone. There'd been no word from Mum either.

'Perhaps she just decided to go home,' Ingrid said, as she put tea-bags into mugs. 'You said yourself that she seemed better.'

'She would have got there by now. And why isn't Dad in?' The kettle clicked off. 'I know I said she was driving me mad, but at least while she was here I knew she was safe.'

'Have you had anything to eat today?' Ingrid put our mugs on the table and sat down. 'Don't tell me you're not hungry. Starving yourself isn't going to help.'

'Did I ever tell you you're a nag?'

'I'll take that as a compliment. Look, Nina, your mum might have been acting a bit strangely lately, but she's probably fine. From what you've told me this week, she's still got all her faculties. She's just gone on a bit of a cleaning frenzy.'

I thought about Mum sitting on a tea towel on my sofa and about her insistence that Dad was having an affair. 'I'm not so sure,' I said slowly. 'She's not her normal self at all, but then neither is Dad, thinking about it. I can't believe he didn't just drop everything and rush down here to get her. Where has he been all day? He can't have gone far. She's got the car.'

Ingrid looked at me and I suspected she was thinking the same as me. Maybe Mum was right and he was having an affair. Neither of us put the thought into words, though.

'Staying here worrying about it isn't going to help,' Ingrid said. 'Why don't you go and get changed and I'll take you out for something to eat?'

'But what if one of them phones?'

'We can divert your phone to my mobile.'

There was a stubborn glint in her eyes and I knew there was no sense in arguing. I had, after all, asked for her help. She was right, anyway — I was starving.

As I stood in the shower a few minutes later, washing away the smell of horses from my skin, I hoped she wouldn't start quizzing me about Stewart Taylor or his son over dinner.

She didn't mention his name until we were on our main course and our third glass of wine. Well, I was on my third glass. Ingrid was driving.

'Oliver's lesson went brilliantly,' I said, avoiding her eyes. 'You were right about him learning to ride. He's already mastered the rising trot.'

'Has he started talking to you?' Ingrid had an uncanny knack of tuning into what I least wanted to talk about, I thought. Or perhaps I was getting as paranoid as my mother.

'A bit,' I said, thinking of the chat we'd had that morning, which had led to Stewart's revelations about his wife. It seemed a long time ago. Mum's disappearance had mucked around with

time. Before Ingrid could ask me anything else, her mobile phone rang and I
nearly choked on my steak.

'You'd better get it. Your mother
might hang up if she hears my voice.'

I picked it up and pressed the answer
button.

'Nina?' For a second, I was so
disappointed that it wasn't Mum that I
didn't recognise the male voice.

'It's Stewart Taylor here. I'm sorry to
bother you on a Saturday night, but it's
urgent. Oliver's run away.'

'Run away?' I heard myself echoing
his words stupidly. 'What do you mean?'

'I just went up to say good night and
he's not there. It struck me that he
might have come over to the stables.
Could you check?'

'Yes, yes, of course.'

'I'll be there in about ten minutes.'
He hung up before I got the chance to
tell him that I was in the pub with
Ingrid and not actually at home.

She raised her eyebrows as I discon-
nected. 'Problems?'

I explained what had happened and ten minutes later we were in her car and driving back towards the stables.

When we got there, Stewart's car was parked outside the gate, which I kept padlocked at night. He looked as though he'd just arrived. As our headlights drew up behind him, he jumped out of his car and slammed the door.

'I'm sorry about that,' I said. 'We were having something to eat up the road.'

He nodded, his face strained and pale.

Ingrid got out of the car. 'What happened?' she asked him. 'Had he been upset or something?'

Stewart didn't answer her. He was already climbing over the gate.

We followed him. It was quicker than opening the padlock. The security lights beamed on as we went across the yard.

'Oliver!' Stewart shouted. 'Are you here?'

There was no answer and even in the

shadowy half-light, I could see the defeat in his shoulders. All the horses were looking over their stable doors, ears flicking at this unexpected late visit. Buska whinnied.

I went across to Stewart. 'It's an awfully long way for a little boy to come, especially in the dark.'

'I couldn't think of anywhere else. And after what happened today . . . ' He didn't seem to care that Ingrid was in earshot. 'God, this is all my fault. I'd never forgive myself if anything happened to him.'

'Let's have a proper look round. He might be here. I'll switch on the stable lights and you can check properly.'

Ingrid was already going into stables, but it occurred to me that if Oliver were here, he wouldn't be in just any stable; he'd be with Leah. I ran to her stable at the end of the yard, my heart hammering adrenaline around my body.

Leah gave a soft whinny of greeting as I slid back the bolt, but I could see without going in that Oliver wasn't there. There was a flattened patch of straw in the corner where Leah must have been lying down, but there was no sign of a little boy.

'Any luck?' Ingrid shouted across the yard.

'No. No sign of him.'

'I'll drive down the lane in my car,' she called. 'He might have got mixed up in the dark and gone into one of the other gates by mistake.'

'Good idea,' I replied, trying not to think of the water-filled ditches that ran along either side of the unmade road. What if Oliver had lost his footing and stumbled into one of them? It was a cold night. He could have hypothermia, or worse. I forced myself to think of something else.

'Are there any more stables? Anywhere else he could be hiding?' Stewart's voice was threaded with panic and for the second time that day I felt desperately sorry for him.

'No more stables.' We stood together

in the middle of the yard. 'There's the bit where we keep the tools.' I pointed and he hurried across, ducking his head to avoid the corrugated iron roof. Oliver surely wouldn't have gone in there, I thought. It was hardly a welcoming hideaway among the pitchforks and the brooms and the spiders.

'Where would I go if I was a child?' I thought. 'On a dark, cold night like this. Where, apart from a horse's stable, might it be warm?'

The answer came quickly. The hay barn that backed on to the horses' boxes. He would know it was there because we passed it on the way to the school where he'd had his lessons. 'I'll just check round the back,' I shouted to Stewart.

There was no light in the barn. I stood at the bottom of the stacked-up bales while my eyes adjusted, the warm sweetness of hay filling my nostrils. 'Oliver,' I called softly. 'Are you in here, love?'

The faintest rustling in the far corner

of the barn. A rat, maybe? Or a frightened child? I scrambled towards the noise and as I did so one of the hay bales moved and I heard a small sob. Then the hay bale toppled forwards and revealed Oliver's hiding place. He must have burrowed down the back of the stack.

'It's all right, lovie.' I climbed over the bales and held out my arms and he came into them. He was shivering all over, I realised, although whether from cold or from fright, I couldn't tell. For a few seconds I was too out of breath with relief to say anything. I just hugged him.

'Is Dad very cross?' he whispered.

'Of course he's not cross. Just worried.'

'I went to see Leah, but she kept walking round and I thought she was going to stand on me.'

He snuggled against me and I lifted him out of the nest he'd dug. 'Come on, lovie, let's go and tell your dad that you're safe.'

'You've obviously made quite an impression on Stewart Taylor, as well as on his son,' Ingrid said. She raised her eyebrows and I shook my head.

'He was just saying thanks.'

'So I saw,' she said drily.

They'd just left, after drinking enough warming hot chocolates in my kitchen to sink a battleship. Oliver had been so drowsy he'd fallen asleep in his father's arms and I'd carried a blanket out to the car to put over him on the back seat. I'd been heading for the front door, which I'd left open, when Stewart had called me back. 'I never apologised for interrupting your meal.'

'Don't be daft.'

'And for this morning too — it helped.'

'Just get him home and don't worry about it.'

'I will. And thanks.' Before I could react, he bent and kissed me on the cheek. Just the lightest, briefest kiss that one friend might give to another. The sort of kiss you couldn't possibly read anything into — unless, of course, you were Ingrid and happened to have witnessed it out of the kitchen window.

'The poor man's light-headed with relief,' I told her now.

'Mmm,' she said. 'Sounded like he was saying thanks for something that happened this morning.'

'Oliver's lesson went well, I told you.' I could feel myself flushing and knew Ingrid would jump to all the wrong conclusions, but without revealing Stewart's secret, there was no way I could defend myself. 'Oliver was a bit upset about his mum,' I said finally. 'He'd got it into his head that it was all his fault she'd left them. I told Stewart that he ought to talk to him. Maybe it was something to do with that.'

She gave me a quick, sharp glance, but all she said, was, 'Yes, you're probably right. 'Well, I think I'd better be making a move too. Did you want to try your dad again before I go?'

I jumped. I'd been so caught up in the evening's events that I'd forgotten all about Mum's disappearance. The second time that day, I thought wryly, that Stewart Taylor's problems had overshadowed mine. I dialled my parents' phone number. At least I could guarantee that Dad would be in at this time of night, even if I had to get him out of bed. I was aware of Ingrid's eyes on me as I held the phone to my ear. After fourteen rings, I put it down again.

'Still not there?' She frowned. 'How long would it take you to drive down there?'

'I could get there and back in a day — but I can't, Ingrid. I can't just drop everything. What about the horses?'

'I could do the horses,' she said calmly. 'It's Sunday tomorrow. Why don't you go and see your dad and get it sorted once and for all?'

'It's lovely of you, but I can't let you do that. What about school?'

'If you didn't get back till Monday

morning, it wouldn't matter. It's only a matter of feeding them and turning them out, isn't it? I can do that before I leave.'

As I still hesitated, she said briskly, 'Anyway, I owe you a favour. You're helping Oliver and I know it might sound strange after tonight, but I think that perhaps this is the best thing that could have happened. At least he and his dad are going to talk now. Really talk. That's all down to you, so the least I can do is babysit that lot over the road while you go and sort your own family out.'

'OK,' I said meekly. 'If you're really sure you don't mind getting up at the crack of dawn?'

'I don't mind at all,' she said, swinging her car keys in her hand. 'See you in the morning, then.'

I smiled at her and felt guiltier than ever that I hadn't been able to tell her what had really happened this morning between Oliver, Stewart and me.

★ ★ ★

The next morning, as I drove to the little Cornish village of Twyerdown, where my parents lived, it struck me that I might arrive to find the house deserted. I'd tried phoning again this morning when Ingrid had turned up, as promised, at the crack of dawn.

There had still been no answer and she'd hovered at my shoulder and said, 'All the more reason for you to go. Come on, after a class of eight-year-olds, I can cope with a handful of horses with my eyes closed.'

'You won't forget to cancel those two lessons I've got booked in and grovel profusely?'

'No problem. I'll tell them you had an unforeseen family emergency — which isn't that far off the truth now your mum and dad have both gone missing.'

By lunch-time, I was just outside Twyerdown. My parents had always had a dream of retiring to the coast. Dad's pension hadn't stretched quite far enough, but they'd managed to get about half an hour from the sea and privately I'd often thought they were much better off in the low-maintenance semi they'd ended up with than some tumbledown cottage that needed a lot doing to it.

Now I was almost there, I found I was curiously reluctant to complete my journey. What if they weren't here? Or worse, what if I walked into the middle of a shouting match? That didn't seem very likely. I couldn't remember ever hearing my father raise his voice, however much Mum bossed. Anyway, maybe Ingrid was right. Maybe she'd simply come to her senses, driven back home and the two of them had unplugged the phone and were having a second honeymoon. That seemed unlikelier still. Even so, I was anxious to put off the moment of truth.

I found a pretty coffee shop and was served a pot of tea in a ceramic pot and a plate of chunky, currant-dotted scones by a chatty, ginger-haired waitress.

'On holiday, are you?' she asked, as I paid.

'I'm visiting my parents,' I murmured. 'In Twyerdown.'

'Oh, do they like it? My mum and dad were thinking of getting a place there.'

I said they'd always seemed happy and hoped fervently that I was right and that I wouldn't arrive to find them dividing up their worldly goods.

'Have a lovely time,' she said, smiling.

I thanked her and decided I could procrastinate no longer. Fifteen minutes later, I was turning into my parents' road. As I pulled up outside their house, I wondered idly which side Margaret Jameson-Smythe lived in. Probably the right-hand house, I decided, as I got out of the car and glanced over the low wall. That had the best-tended garden. Maybe Dad really had been helping her with it.

There were no cars in my parents' driveway, so Mum wasn't here. I felt my heart sinking as I walked up to the front door, aware of the loud crunch of my feet on the gravel. I was about to ring the bell when I saw movement in the kitchen. So there was someone in. Suddenly changing my mind about ringing the bell, I decided I'd nip round to the back door instead. I was halfway over the low wall when the kitchen window opened and a woman leaned out.

'If you've come selling, we're not interested,' she bellowed, in a voice that was as big as she was. 'And I'd thank you to use the path next time. You're treading on the geraniums.'

'Who are you?' I called back, although my voice wasn't as authoritative as I'd have liked, partly because it was such a shock to see a strange woman leaning out of my mother's kitchen window, and partly because I was balanced precariously, one leg one side of the wall and one the other.

'I could ask you the same thing,' she said, her voice belligerent, and I thought, surely this couldn't be her — the woman Dad was supposed to be having an affair with. Surely he wouldn't have moved her in while Mum had been away? It certainly explained his reluctance to come hurrying round to collect her.

'I'm looking for my parents,' I said icily, swinging my leg back over the wall so that I was standing on the front path again.

'Well, why didn't you say so? You're Nina, are you?'

'That's right.'

'Hang on a mo and I'll come round and let you in.'

A minute or so later, she stood huffing at the front door. 'Pleased to meet you, Nina. I'm Maggie from next door.' She held out a large hand, which I ignored.

'Is my father in there?' I asked stiffly.

To my consternation, a grin split her ruddy face. 'Oh my Gawd, not you an' all. No, he's not here.' She stood aside, but there was still only just enough room to squeeze past her into the narrow hallway.

I strode past her into the kitchen and stopped short. My mother was sitting at the kitchen table, looking very pale and very tired, but in control of the situation.

'Hello, Nina,' she said quietly. 'You'd better sit down. I think I've got a bit of explaining to do.'

4

'I'll make myself scarce,' Maggie said from the doorway and my mother nodded. A small, quiet nod.

'You'll let me know if there's news from the hospital?'

'Of course.'

I sat next to Mum at the kitchen table. 'What on earth's going on? I was worried sick when you disappeared. Why didn't you leave me a note or phone, or something?' I could hear the annoyance edging my voice, but I couldn't stop it. The long drive and the worry of the past twenty-four hours were catching up with me. 'And what's this about hospital?'

'If you'll let me get a word in edge-ways, Nina, I'll tell you.' She was pale and there were fine lines of tiredness around her eyes. She looked, I thought uneasily, as if she'd been up all night.

'Your father's had a heart attack,' she said. 'He's all right, but they're keeping him in hospital for a couple of days, just to be sure.'

'A heart attack, my God! Are you sure he's all right? Is that why you rushed off yesterday?'

She pursed her lips. 'I thought you were going to be quiet.'

'Sorry,' I said, chastened by her words, even though there was a part of me that was relieved she was back to her old bossy ways, that she was acting like my mother again.

She started gathering up dirty cups from the table. Then, to my surprise, she stopped, as if suddenly aware of what she was doing. She put the cups back down again and looked at me. 'I decided yesterday morning that whatever had gone wrong between your father and I — well, I wasn't just going to take it lying down. That's partly thanks to you, Nina. I told you off the other day for bottling things up, and it was through telling you that I realised how much I'd been doing the same thing. I'd suspected your father of having an affair, but I'd never told him what I thought.' She hesitated, 'It's hard to know where to start with this. I've been such an idiot. Such a first-class idiot. It's only through talking to Margaret that I've realised how close to the edge I was.'

I was about to interrupt when she put up a hand to stop me. 'Margaret — Maggie — is a psychologist.'

I raised my eyebrows. It was difficult to imagine the huge, shambolic woman I'd just met as a white-coated professional.

'Well, she's retired now, of course, but she used to be. She worked at a woman's prison, you know. She's a very nice lady, actually.'

'You're not making much sense, Mum.'

'Aren't I?' She smiled and I thought that there was something different about her. Something softer, more vulnerable. 'Actually,' she went on, 'I feel that I'm probably making more sense than I've made for a long time, but perhaps I'm telling you this in the wrong order.'

'Go back to why you decided to come home,' I prompted.

She looked irritated for a moment, as if I'd mussed up the order of her thoughts. Then her face cleared. 'Well, I decided that if they were having an affair, I was going to have it out with them. All the way back up here yesterday I was in a furious, bitter rage. I don't think I've ever felt as angry in my entire life as I felt yesterday. Does that make sense?'

I nodded. I knew about anger all right. When Carl had died, I'd been furiously angry. It had seemed so unfair, so wrong. We'd only had three short years with each other and then he'd been snatched from me.

'I was going to kill someone,' Mum went on. 'I'm not sure if it was her or your father, but I was definitely going to kill one of them.'

'Why didn't you tell me?'

'If our positions had been reversed, would you have told me?'

I didn't answer and she inclined her head, raising her eyebrows so that there were four straight lines across her forehead.

'Exactly. We're two of a kind, you and me. Anyway, when I got here, I found your father lying in the hallway. It had just happened. The heart attack. The timing was so unreal, Nina. If I'd been much later . . . ' She tailed off. 'It was a huge shock. The anger was just punched out of me. I . . . I can't tell you.'

As she spoke, I had an image of Dad lying in the hallway, helpless. Although he was such a quiet, unassuming man, I'd always felt he was the stronger of my parents. It hurt to imagine him lying there defenceless.

'Seeing him like that put everything in perspective,' she went on softly. 'I realised that I'd been worrying all that time over losing him, over something that I didn't even know for sure was happening. When I saw him lying in the hallway, it hit me that I really could lose him. For good.' She shuddered. 'I'm sorry I didn't phone you, Nina, but it's been a tough twenty-four hours.' She clenched her hands in her lap and I saw myself in the gesture.

'Oh, Mum,' I said.

'I'm all right. Honestly. In fact, I haven't felt this clear-headed for years. Thanks to Maggie.'

'What on earth's Maggie got to do with it?'

'Well, yesterday, when the ambulance arrived, Maggie came out to see what was going on. And . . . well, to cut a long story short, she came to the hospital with me. We were there most of the night waiting for news on your father and talking.' She leaned back in her chair. 'You ought to talk to her, you know. She's the most amazing person.'

'I don't think I'm in need of a psychologist, Mum.'

She raised her eyebrows. 'Willows

bend in the storm, Nina. It's the tough old oaks like us who break.'

I'd never heard her say anything like that before. The words sounded odd coming from her lips, but I had to admit that, beneath the obvious worry for Dad, there was a new peace in her face.

'Have you been up all night?'

'Most of it, yes.'

'Where's your car?'

'Still at the hospital. I drove us there — we followed the ambulance, but this morning I didn't have the energy to drive back, so we got a taxi.'

'Shall I give you a lift over to get it?'

'Later.' She yawned. 'If you don't mind, Nina, I think I need my bed. I'm absolutely shattered.'

'Of course I don't mind. I'll do the washing-up or something.'

She got up stiffly. 'I shouldn't bother.' There was a smile in her voice. 'There are more important things in life than cleaning.'

An odd thing to say, I thought, seeing

as she'd spent the last week cleaning my bungalow from top to bottom several times a day.

Alone in the kitchen, I made myself a coffee. Poor Dad — and poor Mum. Restless, I went out on to the patio at the back of my parents' house to drink it.

It was while I was out there that Maggie called to me over the fence. 'Like a biscuit to go with that?'

'Aren't you tired? My mother's just gone to bed.'

'No. I've never needed much sleep.' She came across and leaned on the fence, which looked as though it might buckle under her weight. I'd been wrong about which house she lived in. It wasn't the one with the well-tended garden. Her back garden looked as if it needed a flame-thrower to clear it.

'It's much worse in the summer,' she said cheerfully, following my gaze. 'That's why your dad was giving me a hand. Two of us against the brambles instead of one.' She laughed then, and the movement rippled down her huge chest. 'I still can't believe your mum thought we were at it.' Her laughter was infectious and I felt myself relax a bit, but not enough to join her. I was still trying to adjust from the image I'd had of scarlet woman Margaret Jameson-Smythe to the reality of Maggie, the ally, with her big face and her big laugh, who seemed to have gone some way to restoring my mother's sanity.

'Mum turned up on my doorstep last week with a vacuum cleaner and a box full of polishing stuff,' I said to her. 'I wasn't able to prise them out of her hands all week. It was like she was on some sort of cleaning frenzy or something. I was really worried about her . . . ' I broke off and she looked at me, with eyes that were both sharp and kind.

'Perhaps your mum didn't want to face up to what was really bothering her,' she said gently. 'Perhaps that's what it was all about.'

'But do you think she'll be all right

now? Do you think I should get her to see a doctor or something?'

'I think she'll be fine.' She nodded, but more to herself than me. 'She's got everything well and truly in perspective again, I'd say.'

'That's a relief.' I moved a bit closer to the fence.

'She's worried about you, though,' Maggie said unexpectedly.

'Me? What on earth for?'

'She doesn't think you've got over losing your husband.'

I froze. I didn't want to talk about Carl, not here, not to this stranger, however much she might have helped my mother.

'I'm fine,' I said carefully. 'I still miss him, of course I do. But then it's only been a year.'

She didn't say anything else, but something in her expression reminded me of Ingrid when I told her I was fine, although I couldn't put my finger on exactly what.

Later that night, when I drove home,

I thought about what Maggie had said about Mum worrying about me. Did she really think I hadn't got over Carl? Mum's words about us being two of a kind and not able to bend in a storm bothered me, but there hadn't been time to ask her about it. When she'd woken up it had been nearly five and then we'd gone to see Dad.

I'd leaned over the narrow bed and kissed him and thought he looked very well for someone who'd just had a heart attack, if a little gaunt. Mum held his hand the whole time we were there and I'd known from the way that they looked at each other that there'd be no more talk of divorce. Seeing them so close was a relief, but it also made me feel lonely in a way I never felt at home.

Mum had tried to get me to stay the night, but I'd said no, it wasn't fair on Ingrid. Besides, I could see she didn't need me any more. Not like she had. In the hallway, I'd bent to kiss her and to my surprise she put her arms around me and hugged me.

'Be happy, Nina.'

'I am happy,' I'd said. 'Especially now that I know you and Dad are OK.'

'Maybe when he's out of hospital we'll come and visit you. Have a proper holiday in Dorset.'

'On one condition,' I said, extricating myself.

'What's that?'

'You'll leave the vacuum cleaner at home.'

'Lots of daughters would be glad of the help,' she said, but there was a glint of amusement in her eyes.

* * *

'Thank heavens she's all right,' Ingrid said, when I got back just before midnight. I'd said not to bother waiting for me, but she was still there. 'It must be a huge weight off your mind,' she said, studying me.

'It is.'

'You don't look so good, though.'

'Thanks very much.'

93

'You look as though you need a holiday.' There was a speculative gleam in her blue eyes. 'I could look after the horses again, if you like. It's half-term the week after next and I can do my lesson preparation here just as easily as at home.'

'I don't want a holiday.'

She continued as if I hadn't spoken. 'You could go and see Uncle Gustaf. He'd love to see you and you've always said you'd go back to Lapland one day.' She looked at me thoughtfully. 'Carl is still there for you, isn't he? He's still there on that mountainside.'

I was used to her directness, but even so, her words knocked the breath out of me. I didn't remember ever telling Ingrid such a thing, but it was true. For a moment I couldn't speak.

'I can phone him if you like?' she pressed. 'Make some arrangements.' Her clear, blue eyes were gentle. 'It would do you good, Nina.'

I was too tired to argue with her. 'I'll think about it,' I said.

I did think about it over the next few days. I even mentioned it to Mum on one of my phone calls to see how Dad was getting on.

'He's fine. He sends his love,' she said. 'Ingrid's right. It would do you good to have a break, though I can't see why you want to go somewhere freezing cold. Why not go to Spain like everyone else?'

I smiled. Although I felt that Mum and I were closer to understanding each other than we'd ever been, I knew we'd never be on the same wavelength completely.

By the end of the week the idea of going to Kiruna had grown in my mind. Carl had been close to his Uncle Gustaf and had visited him every year, but I'd only gone the once, soon after we were married. Because of the horses, it had been difficult for both of us to get away for long. As Ingrid had predicted, Gustaf said he'd be delighted to see me, but I think I surprised her almost as much as I surprised myself when I said

I'd go, just for a few days. It was illogical, I knew, but Ingrid was right. There was a part of me that believed the only place I'd feel close to Carl was on the mountainside where he'd lost his life.

★ ★ ★

I'd imagined making the journey so many times that there was almost a sense of *déjà vu* as I sat on the plane. I was finally going to get the chance to say my goodbyes. As we began our descent into Kiruna airport, the knot of excitement in my stomach grew and I had the sensation that I was getting steadily closer to Carl.

Uncle Gustaf met me in his husky sled, as arranged. He looked exactly as I remembered. Bearded and stocky with brown, smiley eyes and a voice used to shouting above the noise of the dogs. 'Hope you've got your thermals on, Nina,' he yelled. 'There's not a lot of heating in these things.'

I laughed and battened down my

furry hat and climbed in behind my bags, which Gustaf said was the safest place to sit. We set off, the yelping and barking miraculously silencing as soon as we started to move. Soon there was no sound except for the panting of the dogs and the scrape of the runners over the snow.

'Nowhere else on earth is as beautiful or as peaceful,' Carl had told me, when he'd brought me here. His eyes had sparkled in the clear, arctic light. He'd been so proud of his homeland.

Now I blinked against the wind chill. I'd forgotten how awesomely big it was, and how cold. Snow stretched in all directions, thick duvets of white across the land, broken only by the ubiquitous firs. The wind stung my face as we sped through the black and white landscape and the memories curved in on me, bittersweet. The wild beauty of our surroundings brought tears aching to my throat. But it was too cold for tears. They would have been ice on my face in seconds.

'When you feel ready, I'll take you there,' Gustaf said to me that evening, as we ate arctic char from trays on our laps in the log-fire warmth of his tiny front room. He knew why I'd come. He and Ingrid had discussed it on the phone. I'd thought I'd feel awkward about it, but somehow it was easier to discuss Carl's death in this wild, inhospitable place than it had been at home, in the safe routines of my life. And Gustaf had been with him, after all. They'd been skiing off piste when the accident had happened. He'd been the one who'd called out the air ambulance, even though he'd known as soon as he'd reached his nephew's side that it had been too late for that.

We went after lunch the next day. Gustaf took me on his snowmobile, which he said was more practical than dogs for a journey up a mountain. 'Snowmobiles don't get tired and they don't make a row when you stop them,' he said ruefully.

I'd always thought I'd have some

sense of recognition when I saw the place of Carl's death. Feel something of his presence still lingering. But when Gustaf stopped the snowmobile after an hour or so and pointed towards a belt of trees, I was surprised that we'd arrived.

'I'll wait here,' he said. 'Take as long as you like.'

I tramped through the snow until I reached the trees, cloaked in white, their branches bent beneath the weight. Just beyond them, Gustaf had told me, was the path where it had happened. The path where they'd skied a thousand times before without mishap. I found it as he'd said, winding down between the glittering, snow-clad firs. It looked like every other off-piste path. Icily beautiful, it was like being in some winter fairyland, but this place was just as empty as every other part of the mountain. There was nothing of Carl here. He still felt as far from me as when I stood in the remembrance garden at home. I sank to my knees in the deep snow at the edge of the path and screwed up my eyes against the bitter disappointment. Then I howled my grief into the silence, not caring who heard, not caring about anything any more.

When I came back, Gustaf was stamping his feet in the snow and banging his hands together, his back to me. I touched his shoulder and he turned and looked into my face, his eyes kind. Then, without a word, we got back on the snowmobile and headed down the mountain.

Back in his front room, he sat me in front of the fire and poured me a glass of hot lingonberry juice. For a while neither of us spoke.

'He wasn't there,' I said at last. 'I've always hoped I might find something of him there.'

Gustaf held his hand across his heart and said, 'This is where you'll find him Nina, love. Nowhere else now. This is the only place.'

I began to cry again. He got up and

went out of the room and I thought I'd embarrassed him, but when he came back he was carrying a box of tissues.

'The colder the winter, the thicker the ice gets,' he said gently, putting the box in front of me. 'You have ice around your heart, I think. But when the thaw does come, then the first cracks are the hardest. Do you understand what I am saying?'

I blew my nose. I wasn't sure I did understand, but I could hear the kindness in his voice. It was enough.

★   ★   ★

'Gustaf's right,' Ingrid said. 'We'll always have him in our hearts. You know that, don't you?' She'd picked me up from the airport and we'd stopped in a motorway service station halfway back for coffee.

'Yes, I know.' I looked at her and it struck me that he'll always live on in his sister, too. They looked alike, but they also had the same strength, the same quiet serenity. 'I'm glad I went,' I said. 'Thanks, Ingrid. You were right. I'd kidded myself ever since we lost him that I was fine, when I wasn't really. I guess I'm as bad as my mum.'

'We all kid ourselves a bit,' she said. 'It's human nature. And while we're on the subject of kidding ourselves, I heard a rumour the other day in the staffroom, about Stewart Taylor.' She sighed. 'I heard that his wife was doing three years for fraud and that he was divorcing her.'

I met her eyes above my cup and didn't say anything.

'Hey, you knew that, didn't you?'

'Not the divorce bit.'

'Poor Stewart. Is that why Oliver ran away that time?'

'Yes, I think it was, but he's all right now. Stewart said they'd had a long chat and Oliver's certainly talking a bit more. You were right about him learning to ride.'

'I don't think it's just the riding,' Ingrid said, putting her hand over mine.

'He likes you a lot. They both do.'

I hesitated. 'Stewart asked me if I'd go out for a pizza with them, to say thanks.'

'And what did you say?'

'I said I'd think about it.'

She smiled. 'I think Stewart Taylor would be a good friend to have.'

★ ★ ★

She was probably right about that, too, I thought. It was Saturday tea-time a couple of weeks later and Stewart, Oliver and I were in Valentino's which, according to them, did the best pizza in town. The whole place sparkled with Christmas decorations and every time a waiter came out of the kitchen you could smell wafts of garlic. Our table had a red checked tablecloth and a candle in a Chianti bottle with tinsel wrapped around the base. It was the first time I'd been out for ages with anyone except Ingrid, and I was enjoying their company.

'Ingrid said you'd just been to Lapland,' Stewart said conversationally. 'Oliver and I have always wanted to go there, to see the real Father Christmas — haven't we, mate?'

'Yeah, right,' Oliver said, but he looked interested. 'Did you get to ride on a reindeer, Nina?'

Caught off guard, I blinked. Lapland was the last place I wanted to talk about, but Oliver's eyes were expectant and I knew I couldn't disappoint him. 'No, I didn't ride a reindeer,' I told him, 'but I went on a husky sled.'

'Was it very cold?' he asked, his mouth half full of garlic bread. 'Did you get frostbite in your toes?'

I shook my head. For a moment I was tempted to tell him that I'd got frostbite in my heart, except that, if I was honest, that had happened long before Kiruna and it hadn't been frostbite. It had been ice, as Gustaf had said.

I took a deep breath. 'Lapland is one of the most beautiful places on earth. And one of the most peaceful. That's what my husband used to say. He was born there.'

'Does he still live there, then? Is that why you went? To see him?'

'No, love. He died a little over a year ago. He was in a skiing accident.'

He looked at me, round-eyed. 'Were you very sad? Did you cry?'

'Oliver,' Stewart hushed him. 'Nina doesn't want to talk about that.'

'It's all right.' I smiled at Oliver. 'Yes, I was very sad and yes, I cried and cried, but I'm getting over it now. I'm adjusting.'

To my surprise, it was true. I hadn't found what I'd been expecting to find on that mountainside, but I had found peace. I might not have realised it until today, but I'd also found the courage to move on.

I smiled at both of them. 'So who's having pudding, then?'

'I'm having ice-cream,' Oliver said, studying the menu.

'What do you fancy, Nina?' Stewart asked.

'Something hot, I think. How about you?'

'Apple pie and cream sounds good.'

Oliver snapped the menu shut. 'Strawberry,' he said.

I wasn't the only one to have to adjust, I thought, looking at them. They'd had to make huge adjustments, too, and would have to go on making them. Maybe that was what life was about. Adjusting. I had a feeling Ingrid was right about something else as well. It was easier to do it with friends around you, whatever the future held.

THE END